Libby, Oscar & Me

Libby, Oscar

First published by
Lothian Publishing Company Pty Ltd, Melbourne, Australia

First American Edition published in 1985 by
Peter Bedrick Books,
125 East 23 Street,
New York, NY 10010

ISBN 0-911745-89-0

Library of Congress Catalog Card Number 84-45430

Printed in Hong Kong

& Me

Bob Graham

Bedrick/Blackie

I am Emily. I am a master of disguises.

I can be anyone I want to be.

I can be a
tightrope walker.

I can direct the traffic.

I am a witch.

Libby is my witch's cat

and my cat can be anything she wants to be.

Libby is funny,

Libby is crazy.

Libby hunts parrots.

They waddle around on the garden path,

but they always hear her coming

because I tied a bell around her neck.

Libby likes to curl up on the step

with Oscar and me and sleep in the sun.

Oscar is black and shiny as a seal.

He dives for rocks

and wrestles with old tires

Oscar is my tracker dog.

He *loves* cats, but . . .

Oscar hates big dogs.

They frighten him.

They frighten me too,

and Libby.

Best of all we like Sundays.

I put all my toys in a cart.

I put on a really clever disguise

and off we all go to the park.

If we should meet the dogs from down the road . . .

Oscar pretends he's dead
(Oscar is *very* good at that)

and Libby becomes . . .

. . . a fighter,

a chaser,

a scratcher,

a TIGER.

Then we have our picnic in the park.

I throw bread for the pigeons.

Libby chases the pigeons,

Oscar eats the bread.

Then it is time to go home.

Tomorrow is Monday,
a good day for my plastic nose.